To my three sons, Jonah, Kyle and Ethan,
my teachers about the mysteries of life and love.   CJS

In loving memory of my son Jack.   KF

Proceeds from the sale of this book will go to
bereavement charities, research and education.

Note for Librarians: A cataloguing record for this book is available from Library and Archives
Canada at www.collectionscanada.ca/amicus/index-e.html
ISBN 1-4120-8850-X

Printed in Victoria, BC, Canada. Printed on paper with minimum 30% recycled fibre.
Trafford's print shop runs on "green energy" from solar, wind and other environmentally-friendly power sources.

TRAFFORD
PUBLISHING™

Offices in Canada, USA, Ireland and UK

Book sales for North America and international:
Trafford Publishing, 6E–2333 Government St.,
Victoria, BC V8T 4P4 CANADA
phone 250 383 6864 (toll-free 1 888 232 4444)
fax 250 383 6804; email to orders@trafford.com
Book sales in Europe:
Trafford Publishing (UK) Limited, 9 Park End Street, 2nd Floor
Oxford, UK OX1 1HH UNITED KINGDOM
phone 44 (0)1865 722 113 (local rate 0845 230 9601)
facsimile 44 (0)1865 722 868; info.uk@trafford.com
Order online at:
trafford.com/06-0606

10 9 8 7 6 5 4

Hello, my name is Emma the Elephant. I have two brothers, Edgar and my baby brother Ethan.

I remember when Ethan was in my Momma's tummy. We hugged her big tummy so we could hug Ethan too. We couldn't wait to see him.

One day Momma was very sad and crying. Edgar and I wondered what was wrong? We were scared. Momma and Dadda told us that Ethan was born still. He wasn't breathing and his heart wasn't beating.

We looked at our brother Ethan and touched his cold skin. He looked like he was sleeping, but he was not. We really wished he was sleeping though.

I had so many questions in my head. Why did this happen?

How could this happen in Momma's tummy? How can there be life and then no life?

Did this happen because Momma got angry when I was bothering Edgar until he cried?

Momma said this didn't happen because of anything Edgar or I did. She said it is hard to understand, but sometimes babies live a very short life on Earth and then go back to our home with the Great Loving Spirit.

This place is very beautiful, full of loving light, where we will all be together one day, but not until it is our time.

But I wanted Ethan home with us on Earth now - right now! I wondered if he was scared and all alone. Momma said that Ethan was not alone and that he was with our family who were already there. He can still be with us too, and he shows us this in special ways.

Just then we saw a shooting star fly across the sky. Momma and I believed it was a message from Ethan telling us he was okay.

One day I was so upset I didn't know what to do so I just ran and screamed, ran and screamed!!

I wanted to watch my baby brother grow up, to play and swim with him, and spray water at him from my trunk like Edgar and I do.

I was so angry I kicked the sand and tried to knock over a tree. I was so sad I just sat and cried. I was so scared our family would never be happy again.

Momma and Dadda asked me how I was feeling and said it was okay to cry and feel my feelings. It felt good when they hugged me and said that they loved me.

We had a special service for Ethan. All the children carried purple balloons to where he was buried. We know Ethan was watching and we think he really liked his parade.

Dadda gave Edgar and me a yellow rose to carry and we put it on the little white box where Ethan lay. When I gave him my flower I hoped it would make him alive on Earth again. I was sad when that didn't happen.

I couldn't understand how we could leave Ethan in the white box.

Dadda explained that we only need our bodies on Earth, but who we are, our own ray of light, continues to live on forever. We are all connected to one another through love - always.

It's hard to understand, but somehow I know that Ethan is with us.

After a while we started to think of Ethan without feeling so sad all the time. Each year on the day he was born we make it really special.

Ethan sends a black and white butterfly with baby blue spots to play with us every year.

We call them *Ethan's Butterflies*.

Momma says that no matter how small a baby is or how short a baby's life is, he or she makes a difference and creates even more love in our lives.

We learned that love and life exist forever. So we don't forget Ethan, because we love him.

He is still my brother and always a part of our family.

At first we thought Ethan was lost to the Earth, and to us, but now we know he is not lost to us anymore.

We know he is right beside us whenever we need him. Edgar sometimes stretches his trunk into mid air to pull Ethan close for a big hug when he is sad, frustrated or even when he is happy. I like to run with him – fast!

Ethan loves us and we love him - always and forever.
We know that for sure.

About the Author

Photo by Dale Roddick

Christine Jonas-Simpson's son Ethan William Simpson was born still on July 15, 2001. Her sons, Jonah and Kyle, were 3 and a half years and 22 months old at this time. Christine had difficulty finding a book that reflected her spiritual beliefs, which helped answer her sons' many questions.

This book was inspired by her sons' questions and the spiritual answers that came to Christine, her husband Jack and her sons. Christine is ever grateful for the love and support of her family and friends, including the family of bereaved parents, and especially for the unconditional uplifting love of her sons and husband Jack.

A special thank you to poet and writer, Ronna Bloom, for encouraging the publication of this book and to Karen Friis for bringing the words to life in such a beautiful way. Lastly, she would like to acknowledge Bereaved Families of Ontario (www.bfotoronto.ca) and Perinatal Bereavement Services of Ontario (www.pbso.ca) for the support they offer those who experience the deep loss of a cherished and much loved baby(s).

Christine is a women's health, arts-based researcher and a volunteer who supports bereaved families. She lives in Toronto with her husband, sons and yellow lab, Frodo.

About the Illustrator

Karen's son Jack was born still on September 28, 2004 at 39 weeks old. Karen was devastated by the loss of her first and only child and found a good friend in Christine. She first met the author when Christine was a group facilitator at a local Toronto bereaved families meeting.

Being a Humanist, Karen found few spiritual yet secular books dealing with this subject but felt encouraged by Christine's idea to write this story. Losing her son Jack has inspired Karen, a novice illustrator, to join Christine in this rewarding project.

She is the owner of a small clothing shop and lives in Toronto with her pug, Mavis.